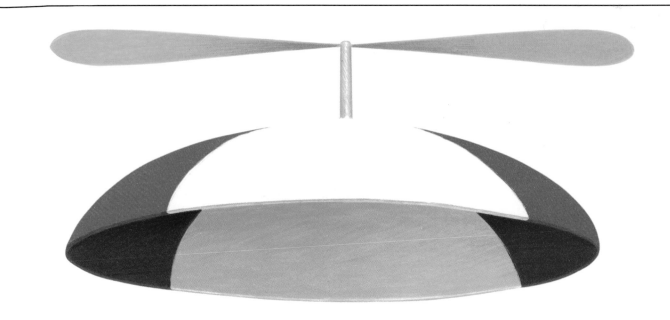

THE ANT BULLY

Story and pictures by JOHN NICKLE

SCHOLASTIC INC.

New York Toronto London Auckland Sydney
Mexico City New Delhi Hong Kong Buenos Aires

ISBN-13: 978-0-439-85116-9
ISBN-10: 0-439-85116-5

12 11 10 9 8 7 6 5 4 3 2 1   6 7 8 9 10 11/0

Printed in the U.S.A.   40

First Bookshelf edition,
July 2006

The illustrations in this book were painted in acrylics. The text type was set in 15-point Base 9. Book design by Kristina Iulo Albertson

TO *Mom and Dad*
FOR GIVING ME THAT FIRST CRAYON
AND TO *Jana*
FOR NOT TAKING IT AWAY.
VERY SPECIAL THANKS TO *Tracy Mack*
FOR MAKING MY STORY BETTER.

Lucas wore funny glasses and a strange hat. Some kids thought he was weird. Sid the neighborhood bully was especially mean to him.

So Lucas bullied the ants.

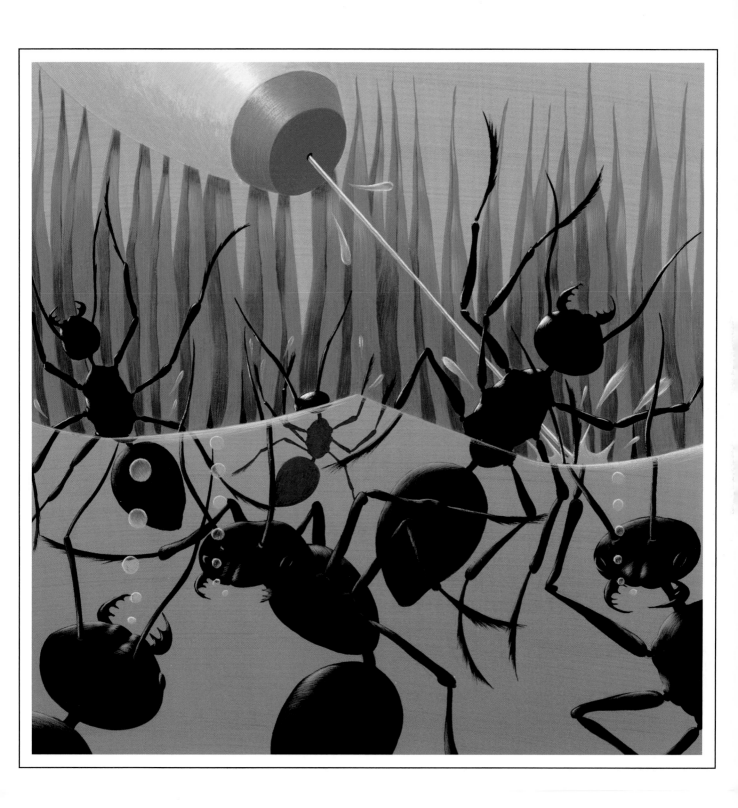

But the ants didn't like to get wet . . .

and soon they had had enough.

With great skill and team effort, they stuffed Lucas's large body into their ant hole and forced him into the Queen's chamber.

Coolly, she looked him over. "So you are the one who always floods my colony. Don't you realize how long and hard we work to build what you destroy in seconds?"

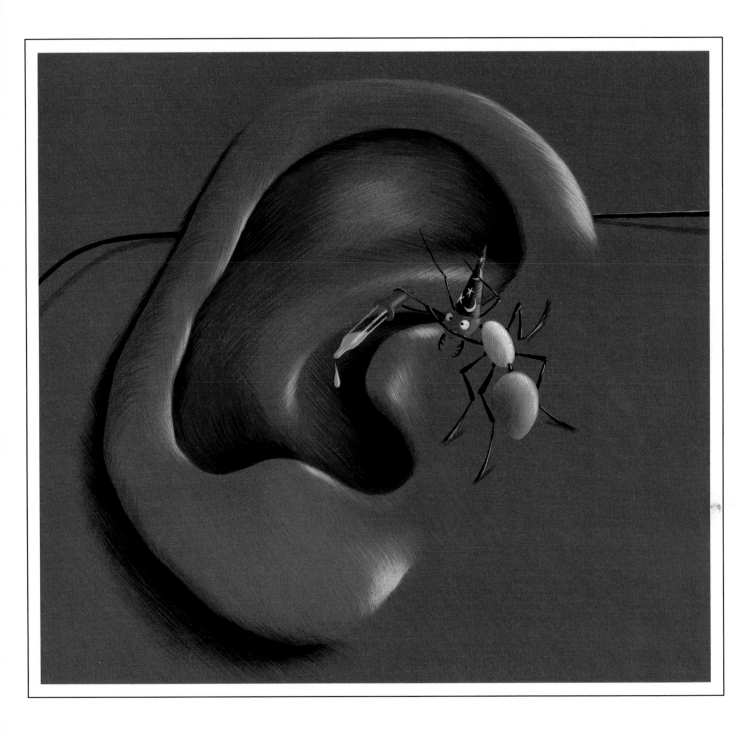

Lucas was too stunned to respond. The Queen took his silence as a further insult. She turned to the Ant Wizard and said, "Shrink this boy! And put him on trial!"

"GUILTY!"

thundered the judge.

Lucas's sentence was harsh . . .

hard labor with the worker ants . . .

gathering food too.

Defending the colony against wasps . . .

and spiders.

But the worst part of his sentence was attending the Queen with the drones.

The Queen, however, was pleased and told Lucas that she would set him free if he passed one final test.

"You must go home and bring me a red Swell Jell."

"But I will need help," Lucas pleaded. "We ants always work together. How else could we gather food, defend ourselves, or please our queen?"

The Queen smiled and said, "Take Speedy and Rene with you. They are upstairs."

As they waited for the cover of night, the two ants had many questions for their new friend.

"What was it like to be a giant?" asked Speedy.

"Were you the biggest giant?" Rene wanted to know.

"I was no giant," replied Lucas. "Not compared with Sid the bully.
He was always stealing my hat and spraying me with the hose."
   "Oh, like you did to us?" said Speedy and Rene together.
   After an awkward silence, the three set out for Lucas's house.

When the last light was turned off, they quietly
snuck into the kitchen to find the Swell Jell.

But just as they were about to make off with their prize,
bright lights flashed and a booming voice filled the room.
"A N N N N T S !" Lucas's father bellowed.

"NO!" Lucas yelled.

His father stopped and looked closer.

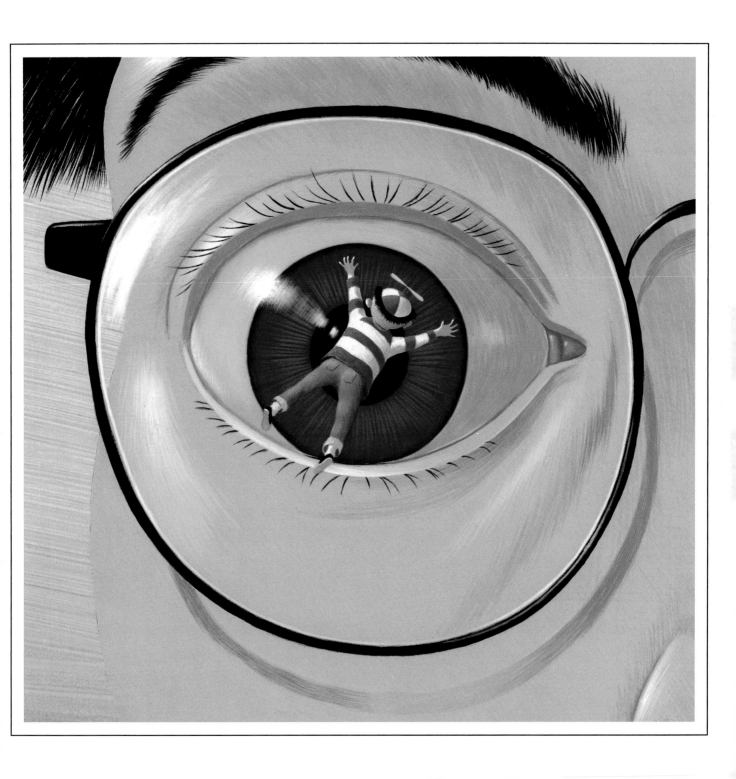

Lucas jumped at his father's face
so Speedy and Rene could escape!

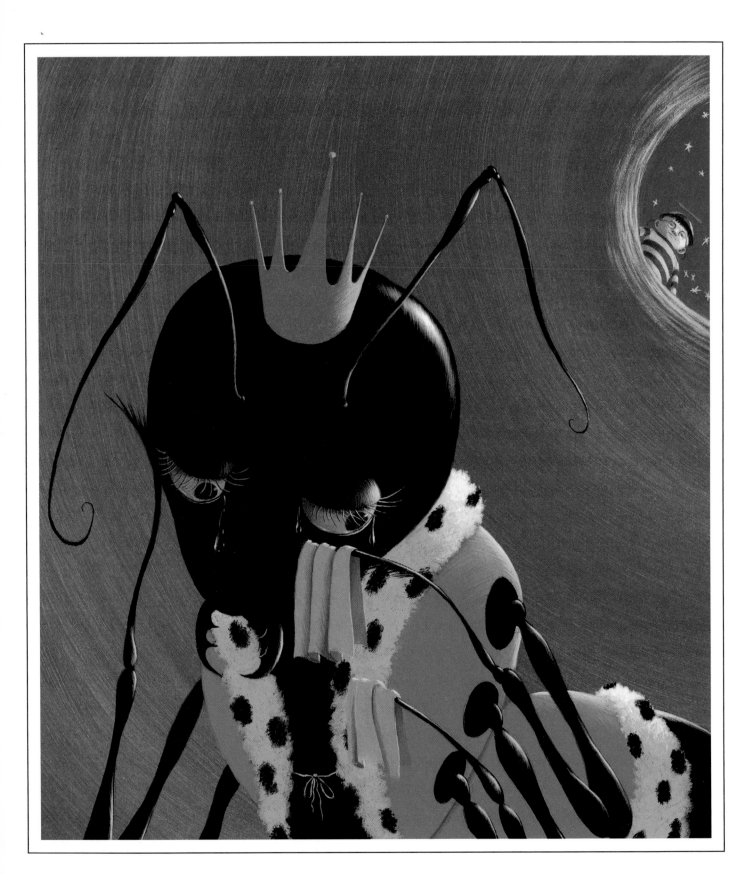

Back at the ant colony, the Queen was very sad. Speedy and Rene had returned, but not Lucas. . . .

Then, to her delight, Lucas arrived! The Queen said, "Young man, you have been so brave, and you have learned the ways of the ants well. Your courage will be rewarded." She told the Ant Wizard to fill his dropper with growth potion.

The wizard trickled potion drops into Lucas's ear until he slowly fell asleep. The ants laid him outside in the tall, soft grass. The next morning, Lucas awoke to an alarming sight.

It was Sid the bully!

But the ants had seen him first.